Reynard's Wonderful Plan

About the story

Reynard thinks about eating up all of Mrs. Pheasant's very tasty friends. He thinks up a very cunning plan to catch them and eat them...

Reynard's Wonderful Plan

Reynard the Fox was hungry. He wanted something to eat. "I'd like two chickens, two ducks, three pheasants, a partridge and a fine fat goose!" he thought. "Now how can I get them? I know – tonight I'll dig a pit outside Mrs. Pheasant's house, and when her friends come to visit her, they'll all fall into it and I shall have a fine feast!"

Reynard dozed in the warm summer sun dreaming of his meal to come. Would it be a nice tender chicken, or a plump partridge – he rather liked the thought of a plump partridge – or would it be a fine fat goose? "Perhaps a little too much to eat all at once," he thought. Ducks, though, they'd make a tasty

dish. "I've always fancied duck for dinner but they might be difficult to catch and they make so much noise with their quack, quacking that they might even warn the others that I'm around. Yes, ducks would be difficult to catch." Dreamily, Reynard the Fox's thoughts rambled on. The warm afternoon turned to dusk, Reynard fell asleep.

A rustle in the grass awoke him – Prickles the Hedgehog was going about his nightly business looking for a tasty grub or two. Reynard the Fox stirred from his slumber. He felt even more hungry by this time.

So that night he dug the hole outside Mrs. Pheasant's house and covered it lightly with twigs and leaves so that no one would see it.

Then he slipped little notes into Mrs. Henny-Penny's letter-box, into Mr. Partridge's, Mrs. Goose's and Mrs. Dilly Duck's asking them to go to breakfast with Mrs. Pheasant and take their families with them.

"Ha, ha!" he thought, "I am a clever fox. When they all come walking to Mrs. Pheasant's tomorrow morning and tumble into my pit, I shall have enough food for breakfast, dinner, and tea for a week!" Reynard the Fox was very pleased with himself.

He sat down underneath a bramble bush to wait for the morning. He felt quite certain that his plan would be very successful.

It was a long night, Reynard the

Fox waited patiently for morning. He began to have some doubts as time went on and he became even more hungry. Morning came at last and Reynard the Fox thought of Mrs. Pheasant's house and the pit he had dug outside it and how one by one Mrs. Pheasant's friends would fall into it.

Mrs. Henny-Penny opened the note, Mr. Partridge opened the note, Mrs. Goose opened the note and so did Mrs. Dilly Duck. Reynard the Fox became even more excited as he thought of his clever plan.

And so it would have been if Mrs. Pheasant had been at home, but she wasn't and everyone knew it. She had gone away to visit

her cousin, Miss. Grouse, who was ill. However, when Mrs. Henny-Penny opened her invitation for a time she had forgotten this.

Mrs. Henny-Penny liked the idea of breakfast with Mrs. Pheasant. She made a good breakfast – fruit juice followed by corn mash. There was always plenty of toast and tea to follow. Would Mrs. Henny-Penny fall for the trap set by Reynard the Fox or would she remember in time that Mrs. Pheasant was away from home visiting her cousin, Miss. Grouse?

She remembered in time. So when Mrs. Henny-Penny and the rest found the invitations in their letter-boxes, supposedly sent by Mrs. Pheasant, they were puzzled. They went round to one another's houses and talked about it.

"Mrs. Pheasant is certainly away," said Mrs. Goose, "so someone else must have sent these invitations. Now why?"

Mrs. Henny-Penny, Mr. Partridge, Mrs. Goose and Mrs. Dilly Duck spent some time reading the invitations. They each passed their invitations round to one another. They looked at the writing – could it have been Mrs. Pheasant's writing? Had she returned from visiting her cousin?

"It's Reynard the Fox!" said Mrs. Henny-Penny suddenly. "He's up to his old tricks! Let's send Prickles the Hedgehog round to Mrs. Pheasant's to see if he's there."

So they did – and Prickles soon saw where Reynard was hiding and found the pit he had dug – and how they chuckled.

Now Prickles the Hedgehog had disturbed Reynard the Fox the night before and had kept a watchful eye on what he was up to. Back he went to the others – and how they chuckled. "Reynard is hiding in wait to

catch you for his dinner," he said. "He has dug a hole in the ground outside Mrs. Pheasant's house and covered it with twigs and leaves, so no-one would see it. He hopes that one of you would fall into it."

"We'll play a trick on him!" they chuckled. So they sent for Mister Dog, and told him what they wanted him to do.

"You must go quietly along the lane to Mrs. Pheasant's," they said, "and when you are nearly there, bark your very, very loudest!"

Mister Dog did as he was told, and just as he got to the bush under which Reynard was waiting, he barked his very loudest, "WUFF! WUFF!WUFF!" Mister Dog thought it was great fun to bark as loud as he could and to scare Reynard the Fox. He had wanted to do this for a long time as Reynard has tried to catch one of his friends before now. Once, Reynard had hidden in a hedge and jumped out nearly catching Mrs. Henny-Penny. Another time he had waited for a long time keeping very still so that Mr. Partridge nearly got caught. Mrs. Dilly Duck and her ducklings also had a lucky escape from Reynard when he tried to swim across to their hideout in the middle of the pond. Reynard did not like the water as it was cold, so he didn't swim out as far as Mrs. Dilly Duck's nest. Another time, when Mrs Goose had wanted to go shopping, Reynard crept up behind her and stole all the eggs in her basket.

"WUFF! WUFF! WUFF!" barked Mister Dog.

Reynard almost jumped out of his skin and fled down the path. He quite forgot about his pit – and crickle-crackle!

He fell through the twigs and leaves that covered it to the hole

below. Then he was trapped. How frightened he was! He tried his hardest to get out, but he couldn't. Then Mister Dog, Mrs. Henny-Penny and the rest all came crowding round the edge and looked down at him.

"Ha, ha!" they said. "Those who dig pits for others fall into them themselves! It serves you right! Ha, ha!"

And all that day different animals came to laugh at Reynard the Fox and he couldn't stop them.

When at last night came and he managed to scramble out, he ran miles away to the mountain that stood high up against the sky. There he found a den for himself, and tried to forget all the laughter he had

heard that day.

Folk say he lives there still – and if they meet him near their farms they don't shoot or shout – they just laugh. And Reynard slinks away with his tail down!

About the Storyteller
Enid Blyton

Enid Blyton wrote poems, stories and plays to amuse herself as a young girl, and after training as a kindergarten teacher she had her first book published.

In all, Enid Blyton wrote around 700 books, including The Famous Five, Malory Towers, The Magic Faraway Tree and Noddy.

Today, her books are available in more than 40 languages and films, television series, video and audio cassettes, CD ROMs and other merchandise, ensuring that she remains the world's favourite children's author.

About the Illustrator
Sylvia A Ward

On leaving school at 15, Sylvia joined County Studio as a trainee illustrator. Over the years she has developed her style of work to include licensed properties for American and UK publishers as well as greeting card and gift wrap designs.

She has designed and produced patterns for Tiffany style stained glass panels. Her hobbies include hand engraving glassware in her own style and design, also collecting curios.